W9-AXU-096

Baby-sitter Blues

by Sarah Willson

Illustrated by Sharon Ross
with Kevin Gallegly

SCHOLASTIC INC.

New York   Toronto   London   Auckland   Sydney
Mexico City   New Delhi   Hong Kong   Buenos Aires

© 2003 Viacom International Inc. All Rights Reserved.
Nickelodeon, Rugrats
and all related titles, logos and characters are
trademarks of Viacom International Inc.

No part of this publication may be reproduced in whole or in part,
or stored in a retrieval system, or transmitted in any form or by any means,
electronic, mechanical, photocopying, recording, or otherwise,
without written permission of the publisher.

Published by Scholastic Inc.,
90 Old Sherman Turnpike, Danbury, Connecticut 06816.

SCHOLASTIC and associated logos are trademarks
and/or registered trademarks of Scholastic Inc.

ISBN 0-439-56281-3

First Scholastic Printing, January 2004

Chapters

"Oh, dear," said Didi Pickles as she hung up the phone. "Taffy is tied up this week. Where will we find a baby-sitter?"

Stu Pickles and all the other dads were away on a fishing trip. The moms had signed up for a one-week class on parenting.

"Try the Lipschitz Institute," suggested Betty DeVille.

"Yes, perhaps they have a graduate student who is looking for experience with children," said Kira Finster.

"Great idea!" said Didi. "We can hire a real expert!"

"Did you hear that?" said Tommy Pickles.
"Taffy got herself all tied up!"

"When's she going to get untied?" asked
his best friend, Chuckie Finster, worriedly.

"That could take ages," said Angelica, Tommy's cousin. "So meanie-while, you babies have a gradual student for a baby-sitter."

"What's a gradual student?" asked Phil DeVille.

"It's someone who's a really slow learner," Angelica replied.

"Well," said Tommy, "since the gradual student is gonna need lots of help learnin' how to baby-sit, it's gonna be our job to teach him!"

"I know all about training baby-sitters," Angelica boasted. "I got lots of 'sperience, 'cause I never have the same one twice. All you gotta do is whine a lot. Then they let you have all the TV and candy you want."

A short time later, the doorbell rang.

"I'm Dwayne," the young man said when Didi opened the door. "I understand you need an expert."

"That's the gradual student," said Kimi
Finster. "He doesn't look like a slow learner."

"He looks like a pushover!" snorted
Angelica. "Pizza cake!"

"I'm writing my thesis on how to train children. In one week, an expert like me can correct all the bad behaviors children have learned from their parents and from inexperienced baby-sitters," Dwayne told the moms.

"Uh-huh!" said Betty. "So, have you ever worked with *actual* kids?"

"Well, no. But I know exactly what I'm doing," Dwayne replied.

He eyed Dil's binky. "I'm sure you mothers mean well, but you just haven't had the proper training. Well, then, see you tomorrow!"

Chapter 3
Bye-bye Binky

The next morning, Dwayne arrived on time.

"Have a wonderful time!" Didi told the babies.

The door closed. Everyone stared up

at Dwayne.

"Ahem! Hello," Dwayne began. "First of all, no more pacifiers." He plucked Dil's binky from his mouth. "Uh, just a second!" he shouted over the wails that erupted from Dil. "I need to see why this baby is crying!" He pulled out a textbook and thumbed through it nervously.

Dil's screams grew louder. Dwayne
frantically searched his book. "Not hungry,
not wet . . . According to the book, he
should not be crying!"

"Why'd he take Dil's binky?" Kimi demanded.

"Remember, he's a slow learner. We gots to teach him how to take care of babies," whispered Tommy. "Don't worry, Dilly. I gots another binky in my diapie."

Dwayne was growing more frustrated. "There's nothing in here about other reasons for crying!" he shouted over Dil's wails. "What do I . . ."

Tommy handed Dil the binky, and his wailing immediately stopped.

"Phew!" said Dwayne with relief. "Well, I suppose a pacifier just this once is okay."

Chapter 4
Angelica's Antics

The next day, Charlotte dropped off Angelica. "Another baby-sitter quit yesterday," Angelica said to the babies. "So I'm stuck here with you guys."

"Today, I will be training the children to eat healthy foods," Dwayne announced to the mothers.

"That's great!" said Didi.

"Lotsa luck," said Betty.

"Leave it to me," Dwayne called to the mothers, as they were going out the door.

"Snack time!" Dwayne said brightly.

"You call that a snack?" said Angelica eyeing a cauliflower.

"Yes," Dwayne replied.

"Watch and learn," Angelica whispered to the babies.

"Can I have a cookie?" Angelica asked, plucking his sleeve.

"No," Dwayne replied calmly.

"Please, can I have a cookie?"

"No."

"Can I have just one? Can I? Huh?"

"No!"

Angelica waited a minute. "Now can I have a cookie?"

"ALL RIGHT!!!!!!" Dwayne shouted.

As Dwayne massaged his aching head, Angelica hurried to the kitchen and returned with a bag of cookies. "It's too easy!" she said with her mouth full.

The babies helped themselves, too.

Chapter 5
Toy Training

A few moments later, Dwayne clapped his textbook shut and sprang to his feet. "Time for positive playskill training!"

"Quick!" Chuckie whispered. "Show him what we like to do, Tommy."

Tommy held up their favorite Reptar video.

Dwayne shuddered. "What are these mothers thinking?" he said. "No videos. *These* are appropriate toys," he said, shaking an ugly puppet.

Chuckie gave a shriek of fright and squeezed under the coffee table.

Dwayne picked up his clipboard and began taking notes. "Prefer . . . watching . . . video . . . of . . . hideous . . . monster," he wrote. Then he hurried off to check his textbook.

"It's okay, Chuckie," Tommy reassured
his friend. "He put away the scary toys. We
can watch Reptar now."

While Dwayne pored over his books,
Angelica joined the babies.

"I think he's slowly learning about babies," said Lil, popping another cookie into her mouth.

"Yeah. Do you think we're trying to teach him too much too fast?" questioned Phil.

"Today I'm going to start teaching the children to read," Dwayne informed the moms the next morning.

"Aren't they a bit young?" asked Kira tentatively.

Dwayne smiled. "Not at all. They just haven't had the proper training," he said, closing the front door.

Turning to the babies, he said seriously, "Today, you must learn to read. If I don't train you kids to do something, my thesis will be ruined!" He pulled out some cards and began taping them up around the room.

"Can I watch TV?" asked Angelica, tugging on Dwayne's sleeve.

"No," he muttered.

"Now can I watch TV?"

"No!"

"Now?"

"NO!!!!!!" Dwayne shouted.

Angelica looked surprised.

"I don't think our baby-sitter training is working too good, Tommy," whispered Chuckie. "When is Taffy going to get herself untied? She lets us watch videos and gives us cookies and doesn't make us eat vegibles."

"But he was doing so well," said Tommy, puzzled.

"Now listen up, kids!" said Dwayne. "Today, there will be no TV, no monster videos, and no sugary snacks!" His voice rose shrilly. "You are going to learn to read, or I will fail my course!"

Everyone stopped and stared at Dwayne.

Chapter 7

Kitchen Chaos

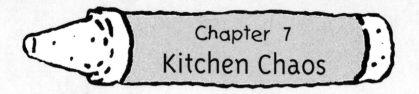

Dwayne opened up his computer and pointed at Angelica. "You, sit down!" he said. "Start learning this reading program while I put up signs for the babies in the kitchen!"

Angelica sat down grumpily at the computer while Dwayne ushered the babies toward the kitchen.

A few minutes later, Angelica called out, "Hey, Dwayne! This is fun! I found a button that makes everything disappear!"

"MY THESIS!" yelled Dwayne, racing out of the kitchen and over to the computer. He began tapping furiously at the keys.

"Now can I watch TV?" asked Angelica sweetly.

Dwayne ignored her and continued banging away frantically.

"He still doesn't understand!" said Lil.

"A baby's gotta do what a baby's gotta do," said Tommy wisely. "Since Dwayne's a slow learner, we gotta really show him what babies like."

"First let's get rid of a few things," Chuckie added. He grabbed a broom and carefully pushed all the educational toys behind the refrigerator.

52

Phil, Lil, and Kimi gathered up all of Dwayne's healthy snacks. Kimi banged on the broccoli with a toy hammer, while Phil dumped the other vegetables into a wagon. Lil poured in water and began mixing.

Dil decorated Dwayne's learning cards with grape juice.

Dwayne staggered into the kitchen, took one look, and howled. "My stuff is wrecked!"

he yelled. "My thesis is erased! You children are . . . UNTRAINABLE!"

Just then the mothers came home.

"Your children don't do what the textbook says they should be doing!" he spluttered at the surprised moms. "I knew I should have gone to law school! I . . . I . . . I *quit!*"

"Oh, dear," said Didi.

The moms and babies watched Dwayne gather up his things and hurry out.

"He seemed a little uptight," chuckled Betty. "Good riddance."

"I'll call and see if Taffy is still tied up," offered Didi.

The next morning, the doorbell rang. And there on the doorstep stood their old baby-sitter Taffy!

"Taffy gotted herself untied!" Tommy declared happily. "Yippee!"

"Oh, Taffy, we're glad to have you back," said Didi, as Taffy came in to greet the kids.

"Can I have a cookie?" Angelica asked hopefully.

Taffy smiled at the kids. "I've got an
idea," she replied. "Let's all go bake some
cookies together!"

The babies and Angelica smiled at Taffy and followed her into the kitchen.

"Where did Dwayne go, anyway?" whispered Chuckie.

"Back to baby-sitter school, I guess," replied Tommy. "He's still gots lots to learn about babies."